BOOK 2

Stewy Baby
and the
Cone of Shame

Kristin Cooper-Herby

Illustrations by Blake Coker

Stewy Baby and the Cone of Shame

Bitterroot Mountain
PUBLISHING

9030 N Hess #331,
Hayden, ID 83835

Illustrations by Blake Coker
Interior Design by Jera Publishing
Editing by Ric Clarke

For permission, please contact
bitterrootmountainpublishing.com

ISBN: Print - 978-1-940025-26-1
ISBN E-book - 978-1-940025-27-8

Printed in the United States of America

To Katie and Cooper
You are my light.

Contents

CHAPTER 1

Stewy Baby

MY NAME IS Stewart-Duke Anna-Belle Campbell. My No. 1 human, Katie, calls me Stewy Baby and I must say I much prefer that. I picked Katie to be my human when I was 8 weeks old. We saw each other in our dreams. I dreamt about a girl with red hair that smelled like maple syrup and she dreamt about a little dog without a tail…ME! The next day, she walked into the barn where I was born and I knew that she was the one. I found her, and she found me and that was that!

We have been living together in the pink palace ever since. I call it the pink palace because everything in the house is pink (even the toilet)! You might say Katie's mom, Kristi, went a little crazy with the color pink when Katie's dad, Dan the Man, built their house. Luckily Dan the Man is color blind. Too bad for me I am not! Not that there's anything wrong with pink; it's just a little bright sometimes.

I live in the pink palace with the Campbell family: Katie, who dreams about things that come true, her older brother, Cooper, who can't decide if he's a super hero or a cowboy. Kristi is Katie and Cooper's mom. She has a delicious dessert business. She spends her days in a big kitchen baking cheese cakes. We love it when the oven decides to "misbehave" because then, we get the burned cheese cakes to eat for ourselves. Dan the Man is the man of the house. He's a builder and has a traveling ski show called Outrageous Air. Last but not least, we have Spud the

cat. Spud and I didn't much care for each other at first, but we are learning to tolerate one another.

I'm lucky enough to have grandparent humans too. Kristi's mom, MiMi, is my very favorite grandparent human. She takes me and the kids once a week and we go on all sorts of adventures. Yesterday she took us to a park where I got to chase birds into the water. There were hundreds of white birds that MiMi called seagulls. She said they were nasty, dirty birds so I chased them away. MiMi is married to my Grandpa Tom. The first time I met Grandpa Tom he said I had "goat eyes." I didn't care for that comment much, but I know now that Grandpa Tom is a good human. If I could talk I would tell Grandpa Tom that I would rather have "goat eyes" than horse teeth! My other human grandma is Grandma Marlene, Dan's mom. Katie says she's the queen of clean and doesn't like to get dirty.

So that's why I shouldn't sit in her lap or lick her face. I've only met her once, and she seemed very nice. I tried my very best not to jump on her and get her dirty. She said I was a good puppy, gave me a Milk Bone, and then washed her hands.

Ed the Magpie is the neighborhood pest. He is a big black and white bird that always tries to get me into trouble. Ed is a pesky magpie. He says he's much smarter than his cousin the crow, but I'm not sure I believe him. One thing is for sure, he is much more annoying. He does horrible things and tries to blame them on me! Once he even talked me into escaping and getting into people's garbage cans. I was just a puppy then and not very smart. I'm much smarter now. I'm a whopping 3 months old. I have been living in the pink palace for one whole month!

We live next door to really nice neighbors, Pajama Pam, and her husband, Big

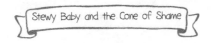

Harold. I call Pam, Pajama Pam, because she always wears her pajamas no matter what time of day it is. I call Harold, Big Harold, because… you guessed it, he's a big, tall guy! Pajama Pam talks to me through the fence every day and usually slips me some sort of yummy snacks. Yesterday she gave me a pulled pork sandwich. The day before she gave me a cupcake. I'm not supposed to have human food because it gives me a bad case of the wind. But I love it so much I just can't help myself.

I have learned three very important things since living in the pink palace

1. Underwear is fun to chew
2. Shoes are delicious — especially flip flops.
3. Garbage cans are meant for garbage, not puppies.

I know I shouldn't chew on anything, but my darned puppy teeth are falling out and my large canine teeth are growing in. The only thing that makes them feel better is chewing on things. Lately, Cooper has been giving me ice cubes to chew on and that seems to help.

Man oh man, do I love my life.

CHAPTER 2

The Great Pink Porcelean Throne

I T WAS MY favorite day of the week; Saturday! Ever since I arrived at the pink palace, we had a tradition, every Saturday Dan, Katie and I would get up early while Kristi and Cooper slept in. Dan the Man would make breakfast and Katie and I would eat it. Then Katie would read the comics to me from the The Coeur d'Alene Press newspaper.

Every morning when Katie wakes up, she always does the same thing. She yawns and stretches, gets out of bed and stumbles to what she calls "MOMMY'S

BATHROOM." It has a big pink bath-tub, matching pink sinks and what else? A pink toilet. The toilet is the thing I don't understand. Dogs, cats, birds, cows, even horses do their potties outside. Why can't humans? The pink palace has a big enough backyard to hold lots of potty but they all insist on going inside. It's the strangest thing I have ever seen. Every morning, afternoon and night Katie does her potties on the pink toilet then she pulls a lever and whoosh, the potties disappear. I think they go into the backyard. Wouldn't it be easier to just go potty there in the first place? It truly baffles me.

Katie tried to explain what she was doing on one of my first mornings at her house. I must have looked at her funny when she sat on the toilet because she said:

"Why are you looking at me that way Stewy?"

I cocked my head to one side and barked at her. If only I could talk I would have said, "Katie, you know I love you but why on earth do you do your potties on that silly pink toilet when you have a perfectly good lawn out back?"

I swear Katie understands me most of the time because she said, "Oh, you're probably wondering why I'm going potty on this silly pink contraption. This is called a toilet and it's where humans go to the bathroom. You go outside because you can't use a toilet."

I still didn't get it. I trotted downstairs to see if Dan the Man was feeling extra nice that morning and wanted to share his breakfast with me.

"Good morning Stewy Bear," Dan the Man said. "Do you want to have a little bite of my bacon and eggs on your kibbles?"

Does Katie do her potties on the pink toilet? Duh! Did I ever. I barked once and spun around in a little circle.

"I saved some bacon grease to driz-zle on the top for you. Don't tell Kristi though. She says you're going to get fat if I keep feeding you human food," Dan said as he poured hot bacon grease

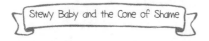

on my kibbles. He topped it with some scrambled eggs and bacon. I felt a drop of drool drip from my mouth. Human food was the best! I don't understand why Mike the vet said I shouldn't have it. It does tend to give me a bad case of the wind but that's just who I am. Kristi said she's used to it. She grew up with her brother, Kevin, who was also well known for his gas. She said it's his claim to fame, whatever that means.

"There you go good girl," Dan said as he placed my bowl on the floor. "It's still hot, so wait for it to cool."

Dan the Man and I did not get off to the best start in our relationship. Kristi, Katie and Cooper brought me home without checking with Dan the Man first so we were all in trouble for a while. Luckily, Dan's bark is worse than his bite and we have become great friends (especially when he gives me bacon grease).

I sat at my bowl and drooled and drooled. I didn't want to burn my tongue again like I did the first time I ate bacon grease. I couldn't taste anything for weeks. I looked at Dan and waited. He always gave me the okay.

"Okay Stewy, it should be cooled off by now." Dan gave me the nod of approval.

I gobbled that tasty bowl down as fast as my canine teeth would let me. There was nothing like a good bowl of kibbles and bacon grease!

"Spud, don't look at Stewart that way! You know that you can't eat bacon grease. Maybe Kristi will give you some tuna juice today," Dan the Man said.

Spud always gave me stink eye and I know exactly why! It was because he used to be the baby of the family and now he has to share his humans with me. I don't speak cat and don't intend to learn because my canine mom, Lucky, told me that cats were

awful, filthy animals. Why were humans and animals always telling me that other animals were filthy? Did humans call me filthy behind my back? I was pretty sure that Grandma Marlene thought of me as filthy.

"Where's Katie Stewart?" Dan asked.

I looked upstairs and barked.

"Ohhhh. Is she still doing her morning doody? She would stay on that thing all day if we let her." Dan turned and yelled up the stairs, "Hey Princess Potty, get off your great pink porcelain throne and come and eat some bacon and eggs!"

Dan the Man really cracks me up!

CHAPTER 3

Walkin Shoes

K RISTI CAME HOME early on Thursday afternoons to spend "quality" time with the kids. Most of the time, Kristi made it home before Katie and Cooper. Every now and then she would arrive a few minutes late so the kids would walk home from the bus stop, lock themselves inside the house and wait patiently for Kristi. This particular Thursday was a late one for Kristi. Katie and Cooper had just come screeching through the front door. I had been alone inside the house for quite some time. I'm not sure how long it was in human hours but in dog hours it was about 49 hours. Forty-nine hours is a doggone long time to sit inside and do nothing.

"Hi Stewy Baby," Katie said as she raced up the stairs doing her potty dance. "I'll give you loves in a minute but I really have to go potty."

Boy did I feel her pain. Try going 49 dog hours without going potty. Good thing I had a nice strong bladder. That's probably why I was able to stay in the pink palace and remain a part of my human's family. I only had one accident in my whole puppy life and that was because I was left inside for over 100 dog hours!

Dan the Man said Katie has the smallest bladder on the planet.

"Everything she drinks goes right through her," Dan the Man said. "Just wait until you go on a road trip with her. It takes us twice as long to get there because we have to stop and go potty so often."

Cooper plopped himself in front of the television. I knew he was a lost cause, so I followed Katie upstairs and sure enough she was settled in on her pink throne.

"Hi Stewy, how was your day good girl?" Katie squealed in her best doggy talk.

I barked at her and tried to do my best imitation of her potty dance to let her know that I too would like to release my potty. Better yet, I would like to go on a walk and release my potty in the big vacant field across the street. The only thing better than kibbles with bacon grease was going on a nice long walk! I raced to Katie's closet and retrieved her stinky tennis shoe. I put it in my mouth and ran to the bathroom. Of course Katie was still on the pink throne. She was singing her favorite princess song. I pranced over to her, lifted my head and dropped her tennis shoe in her lap.

"What's this?" Katie asked.

What the heck did she think it was? It was her stinky tennis shoe! I barked at her and cocked my head.

"This is my tennis shoe! Why did you bring me my tennis shoe?"

I barked again, walked over to her, picked up the stinky tennis shoe, and then dropped it in her lap once more. I backed away, looked at the shoe, then at Katie then barked again. Oh, if only I could talk.

"Do you want to go on a walk good girl?" Katie asked.

Sometimes humans ask the silliest questions. Do you like to sit on that pink porcelain throne? Of course I wanted to go on a walk! I barked and spun around in a circle.

"Wow, wait until I tell Mommy about this one!" Katie said. "You are scary smart!" Katie handed me her shoe, got off the pink throne laughing and said, "Okay Stewy Baby you win! Let's go on a walk!"

Katie walked to her closet and pulled out her other stinky tennis shoe. Guess what color they were? You got it, pink!

"Let me just put my other shoe on and we'll be on our way as soon as Mommy gets home," Katie said. "Spuuuuudddd. Here kitty, kitty, kitty. Do you want to go on a walk too?"

Why did my humans always have to include Spud on our walks? Spud was a cat, not a dog. Dogs walk, cats kill birds. But not Spud, nooooooo. He liked to tag along about 50 yards behind us sneaking from bush to bush. He thought we didn't notice that he was tagging along but we always noticed. Everyone noticed.

Spud yawned, stretched and jumped off the bed. He walked over to Katie and meowed.

Great, I thought. I don't speak cat but I knew that meow meant yes!

"Hi Everyone, I'm home! Sorry I was late but my darn oven was acting up again and I couldn't get my cheesecakes to bake." Kristi hollered as she ran up the stairs.

"Mommy, you're late! Stewy needs to go for a walk; she even got my walking shoes for me!" Katie said.

"Okay, let me just go potty and we'll go," Krisiti replied to Katie.

The apple does not fall far from the tree.

CHAPTER 4

Wiener Dogs?

AS WE WALKED out the front door onto the porch Kristi waved to Pajama Pam. It was 4:00 in the afternoon and sure enough Pajama Pam was wearing her favorite pajamas. They were bright blue with brown dachshunds on them.

"Well hello there, I see you're taking the whole family on a walk again," Pam said looking at the five of us.

"Oh yeah, Spud thinks we don't notice but I know he likes to tag along too," Kristi said.

"You do have a funny bunch of animals. I was just telling Harold that I think we need a couple of dogs of our own. Seems awfully lonely since Red passed away," Pajama Pam said.

"Pam, you can borrow Stewy Baby anytime you need some doggy love!" Katie said.

"Ohhhhhhh thanks. Stewart and I have a special bond don't we Stewart?" Pam said.

I barked twice to agree with Pajama Pam. I was really hoping she would keep all of the special treats a secret.

"Yeeeessss we do but I really want a dog or two of my own," Pajama Pam said.

"What kind of dogs are you thinking about?" Kristi asked. "Another Irish Setter like Red?"

"No, not another Irish Setter. Red was a good dog but I would really like a couple of wiener dogs," Pajama Pam said.

"You mean dachshunds? Why on earth would you want a couple of dachshunds?" Kristi asked.

"You got a thing against dachshunds?" Pam asked.

"I grew up with dachshunds," Kristi said. "I like all dogs, although I do remember that dachshunds were very high maintenance. They barked a lot and ruined my parent's carpet. We had to replace it twice."

"Now don't go telling Harold that," Pajama Pam said. "I have him talked into one and I almost have him talked into two. We're German you know, German humans need German dogs!"

"Oh my gosh, Pam, I had a dream the other night that you got three wiener dogs" Katie exclaimed. "The wiener dogs are your special dogs, Pam, just like Stewy, is my special dog."

"You don't say? I tell you what Katie, come on over tonight and tell Harold about your dream," Pam said.

"Oh no, I believe that Katie will stay out of this one. You're a brave woman, Pam. If I would have brought home a wiener dog we would both be on the street," Kristi said.

"I hope you don't get a wiener dog, Pam, Dad doesn't like small dogs. He calls them rat dogs," Cooper said.

"Well that's not very nice," Pam huffed. "I'll let them know to stay away from Dan- Dan the grumpy man. You know, I'm surprised your dad doesn't like small dogs, he's always reminded me of a Jack Russell Terrier!"

Kristi laughed and said, "Somehow, I don't think Dan would take that as a compliment! Let's just keep that one to ourselves."

"Oh, you know how good I am at keeping secrets!" Pam winked at both of us. If I had a tail, I would have put it between my legs. "You all have a nice walk and, Stewart, don't you worry, I can keep a secret."

I gave Pajama Pam an approving bark and trotted down the street with the Campbell gang—Katie, in a pink tutu spinning circles with her hands in the air, Cooper, running in his cowboy boots and cape, Kristi, singing a happy song and Spud the cat trailing behind us. We were quite the sight!

CHAPTER 5

Ed and Margie

THE BEST THING about the pink palace was that we lived right across the street from a field. Kristi would keep me on my pink leash until we got into the field and away from the neighbors then she would set me free to do my business and run to my little heart's content.

"Hey Stewart what cha doin'?" Ed squawked at me flying very close to my head.

It was bad enough that Spud had to come along on our walk but I really had to draw the line at having Ed the Magpie join us.

"Leave us alone Ed," I barked at him. "Haven't you caused enough trouble?"

"Ya mean the garbage deal-e-o? That was all just fun and games. Besides, that was a long time ago. Forgive and forget Stewart, forgive and forget!" Ed squawked.

I glanced around to make sure that Kristi and the kids didn't see me talking to Ed. I didn't want them to think I would hang out with a Magpie. Luckily, Kristi and Katie had been distracted by some wildflowers. They were trying to figure out a way to get them out of the ground without getting their clothes dirty.

"Coop, run on home and grab a shovel and a bucket. I want to transplant some of these beautiful poppies into our yard," Kristi yelled to Cooper.

"Super Cooper is on it!" Cooper ran past me speedy quick. He didn't even notice Ed.

"Where have you been anyhow? I thought maybe you left town for good. You know, Pajama Pam and Big Harold saw us that day," I barked.

"Yeah, yeah, I know. That's why I flew the coop. I had to fly low for a while. You hang around a neighborhood too long and you never know when ya might get a bb in the butt! Besides, I found myself a hot date!" Ed said.

"A hot date, what's that?" I asked.

"A girl Stewart, a girl! What, were ya born yesterday?" Ed cawed.

"As a matter of fact, Ed, I'm 3 months old! I've grown up a lot and I'm onto your bird games," I barked.

"Hey. No hard feelings, no hard feelings! I just wanted ta introduce my new girl to ya!" Ed said.

Another Magpie that was almost identical to Ed, but a bit smaller flew very close to my head and landed in the field a short distance from me.

"Stewart, meet Margie! Got hitched last week and we're hoping ta have a family this spring. My life has changed forever,"

Ed said in a sad squawk. "This is the one I was tellin' ya about Margie baby. This is Stewart."

"Hey Stewart. Nice ta meet cha. Ed has told me all about your garbage adventure. Says it was one of the best days of his life," Margie squawked in an equally annoying voice.

"Hey Margie," I said rather reluctantly. "Congratulations on the marriage. As far as the garbage adventure goes, I got into a lot of trouble for that one." I didn't trust Ed and I wasn't sure I trusted Margie either.

"Awe Stewart, let it go, let it go," Ed chimed in. "So Stewart, we're lookin' for a place ta call home. Can't live in a bad neighborhood forever ya know."

"I thought you said magpies didn't live in bad neighborhoods," I said.

"Did I say that?" Ed asked.

"Yes, you did. You said that only crows live in bad neighborhoods," I said.

"Yeah well, what can I say? We visit them on occasion alright? So, I promised old Margie here that I would give her a nice neighborhood to raise her kids. I was thinkin' that since you and me get along so well, maybe we could build a home in that big pine tree ya got in the back yard. Ya know the one you was lyin' under the first time we met," Ed squawked.

I glanced at Ed and I glanced at Margie. Margie did seem sort of nice. She gave me her best magpie smile and flew away. "I don't know, Ed. I don't know if Dan the Man would like you hanging out in his tree. He's not very fond of crows," I said.

"Geez kid, cut me some slack. How many times do I has ta tell ya, I am not a crow, I'm a magpie!" Ed said.

"Well, even if Dan let you stay, I don't know that Spud would like it," I said.

Ed was marching back and forth on the ground in front of me, obviously

very focused on finding a new home for his bride and family to be. He was generally very alert to his surroundings but he had a lot on his mind. "Spud? Who's Spud?" Ed asked.

"Our cat!" I barked.

And with that Spud came running out from behind a tree and pounced on Ed.

"What the heck?" Ed squawked as he flew away, narrowly escaping Spud's chompers.

"Sorry Ed!" I said laughing.

If I could have given Spud a high five I would have. I was hoping that he was hiding behind a tree nearby and being sneaky. I knew that he liked magpies even less than I did and I wanted to get even with Ed for our garbage adventure. I didn't want Spud to kill Ed, or even hurt Ed. I just wanted him to give Ed a little scare. I looked at Spud and he looked at me. He had two of Ed's tail feathers in his mouth. I barked as if to say thank you, and he yowled a low

wail. For the first time since I had become a part of Kristi's family, Spud and I had finally connected.

Spud was looking off into the distance and growling. I saw Margie picking through a piece of garbage, oblivious to Charlie, the neighborhood bully that stalked her. Even Spud didn't get along with Charlie the cat. I barked to warn Margie, but she didn't hear me. Charlie was getting closer and he was ready to make his move. I ran as fast as my puppy paws would carry me and cut Charlie off just as he was pouncing on Margie. Margie squawked and flew straight up into the air. I collided with Charlie just as he was getting ready to chomp down on a delicious magpie. He got my skull instead. I yipped! Cat bites hurt!

"Oh my gosh, what's the matter, Stewy Baby?" Katie came rushing to my side. Charlie ran to a nearby tree and climbed to the highest branch.

"Awesome, did you see that? That cat was trying to eat that magpie and Stewy saved it." Cooper was talking very fast, while waving his shovel in the air. "I should give Stewy my super hero cape the way she leaped in the air and saved that bird. It was soooooooo cool."

"What the heck happened?" Kristi asked breathlessly as she came running over to us holding a handful of bright orange flowers.

"Stewy's a hero, she saved her friend!" Katie exclaimed.

"What friend?" Kristi asked.

"Silly Mommy, her magpie friend. That mean cat Charlie was trying to eat it." Katie pointed to the tree that Charlie was hiding in.

"Just when he was leaping into the air to pounce the bird, Stewy flew through the air and took him out. I'm not sure why Stewy yelped. I think it just scared her," Cooper exclaimed.

Katie was on the ground consoling me. I looked up at the tree and saw Charlie glaring at me. Ed and Margie were nowhere to be found.

Spud rubbed against Kristi's legs and yowled.

"Spud doesn't like that cat," Katie explained. "He always beats Spud up. Now, Stewy doesn't like him either."

"I wish I had a slingshot, I'd pop him one right between the eyes," Cooper said.

"Nobody will be popping anybody, anywhere," Kristi scolded.

"Look Stewy, I found one pink poppy among the bunch. This is your reward for being brave!" Katie tucked the flower into my pink collar. "Now nobody will mistake you for a boy!"

"So, why did I go home to get the shovel?" Cooper asked.

"They pulled right out of the ground! Who knew?" Katie laughed.

I sure loved all of the attention that I was getting, but my head kind of hurt. I think Charlie may have chomped me a good one. I had to be brave though for my humans.

We all walked home together. Even Spud walked with us and not behind us. We had definitely made some progress today.

"Hi gang," Mr. Camp our neighbor said, waving as we walked by. "Nice looking bunch of flowers you have there."

"Aren't they beautiful? I found them in the field. I had no idea we had wild poppies here," Kristi replied.

"They're beautiful all right!" Mr. Camp said.

I barked and wagged my nub hoping that Mr. Camp would notice my pretty pink poppy.

"Hey boy, you sure are getting big!" Mr. Camp said stroking my neck.

I bowed my head in shame. Even with a beautiful pink flower in my collar I was still mistaken for a boy!

"Stewy's a girl, Mr. Camp, she's just kind of a tomboy!" Katie said defending me.

"That's right; you are a girl aren't you? We'll of course you are! Look at that pretty pink collar with the matching pink flower. Of course you're a girl!" Mr. Camp said to me.

I licked his hand in appreciation. My nub wagged back and forth as fast it could possibly go! Yes! I was a girl with a pretty pink poppy!

CHAPTER 6

Love Nest

THE NEXT DAY I was in the backyard minding my own business when Ed and Margie swooped over my head and landed in the big pine tree.

"Hey Stewart, what was the big idea with that mangy cat yesterday? I can't believe you almost let him eat me!" Ed was perched on his favorite branch in the big pine tree. Sitting beside him was Margie.

"Yeah Stewart, I thought cha was our friend. What would I have done if the father of my babies had gotten eaten?" Margie squeaked.

"Oh, I wasn't going to let Spud eat you, Ed. I just thought I would let him scare you a bit," I laughed.

"Yeah, yeah. I'll have you know, Stewart, that it just so happens that two of my best, longest tail feathers ended up in his mouth," Ed squawked as he marched back and forth on the branch. His head was bobbing up and down and I couldn't help but notice that he too had a nub.

"I really am sorry about that, Ed. Don't worry; you'll grow new tail feathers," I said. "Besides, Ed, nubs aren't so bad."

"Are ya kiddin' me kid? I've been grooming those babies my entire life. They was my pride and joy. In fact that's what attracted old Margie baby to me in the first place. Aint that right Margie?" Ed said.

"Oh yeah," Margie sighed. "Ed had the nicest tail feathers in the entire trailer park!"

"Okay, Ed, I'm sorry Spud got your tail feathers, but what about the fact that I

saved Margie from Charlie, the neighbor-hood bully."

"Whadaya mean ya saved her? You saved her tail feathers, otherwise, we would both be flyin' around with nubs," Ed complained.

"Charlie wasn't just after Margie's tail feathers, Ed. He wanted to eat Margie for lunch," I said.

"Oh goodness, Stewart, do ya mean ta tell me that you saved my life?" Margie asked in a high pitched squawk.

"Well, let's just say my head stopped him from getting you," I rubbed my head with my paw. It still hurt and a big lump was starting to form. "I took a good chomp to the skull."

"Oh my goodness, Stewart, I thought that was just a smart bump. It's growin' bigger by the minute." Margie was now sitting on my head looking at my bump.

"Would you two stop. Stewart is a dog. She'll be fine, she'll be fine. Let's put the past behind us and start lookin' towards the future. So whadda ya say Stewart? Ya think Dan the Man would care if we camped out in this big tree for a while. Margie's naggin' me about building her a home," Ed squawked.

"Here's the thing, Ed." I said. "Even if Dan the Man didn't mind if you built a home in his tree, I think Spud would mind terribly. You were able to get away from Spud but the babies may not be so fast," I said.

"Oh my gawd, Ed. The dawg has a point. What if that filthy cat tried ta eat our babies?" Margie said.

"He is really good at climbing trees," I said.

"Now ya listen here, mister. Ya promised me a better life. Ya promised me that we would never go back to the trailer park. I has been very patient for two days and I am through! Ya got that?" Margie ruffled her tail feathers and moved her chest back and forth as she scolded Ed.

Poor Ed, he looked like a broken bird. Ever since he got married he just wasn't quite the same. I kind of felt sorry for him.

"Hey, I have an idea," I said.

"Yeah? Well it better be a good one, it better be a darn good one, is all I can say," Ed squawked.

"Look at the tree next door in Pajama Pam and Big Harold's back yard. It's not quite as big as our tree, but it's got to be a step up from the old neighborhood!" I said.

" We're not talkin' about the old neighborhood anymore!" Ed said flying away.

"The kid has a point!" Margie said. "They got any cats or dogs over there?" Margie asked.

"Nope," I said. I didn't dare tell them that Pajama Pam was thinking about getting yippy wiener dogs.

Ed flew back and landed on the branch next to Margie. "The kid is right Babe, it's a nice tree, and there's no sign of anyone else livin' there. I say we start building our new love nest. Then it will be ready for us in the spring. What branch do ya wanna be on?"

"Oh Ed, I could just kiss ya! I kindda like the looks of that big branch near the top. Whadda ya think?" Margie said as she hopped closer to Ed.

"We're on the same page, Margie baby, the same page indeed! The big branch it is!" Ed said.

"Thank you, Stewart. That was a brilliant idea! It's gonna be nice havin' ya as a neighbor! Take care of your skull."

And with that, Ed and Margie flew away to start building their new love nest in Pajama Pam and Big Harold's backyard.

CHAPTER 7

A Third Eye

"**M**OM, CHECK OUT Stewy's smart bump. It's getting really big." Cooper said as he munched on his Cheerios.

The Campbell's always said I was so smart. I had a smart bump on my head to prove it. I had no idea what that meant. I just knew that my head was starting to really hurt and I was pretty sure it wasn't caused by my smart bump.

"Oh my gosh, I just remembered. I had a dream that Stewy had to go see Dr. Mike." Katie was spreading peanut butter on her piece of toast. Peanut butter was my favorite and even that didn't sound good.

Kristi looked up from doing the dishes. "You had a dream about it? I hope she doesn't have to go see Dr. Mike. Come here Stewy Baby, let's take a look at your head."

I reluctantly walked over to Kristi. I knew she was going to touch my bump and I knew it would hurt. "Oh my goodness, Stewy, what happened?" Sure enough, she pressed on my large bump trying to figure out the problem. I let out a yelp because it hurt like crazy!

"Is she going to be okay Mommy?" Katie cried. She had stopped eating her peanut butter toast and was sitting beside me on the kitchen floor.

"Yes honey, don't worry. I think she just has a little owie. I'll make an appointment with Dr. Mike," Kristi reassured Katie.

"Don't worry Kate, Dad says Stewy's tough. Dr. Mike will fix her up." Cooper continued to eat his Cheerios, apparently not worried about my throbbing skull.

I whined and laid my head in Katie's lap. The first time I went to see Dr. Mike he poked me with something sharp a few times. Katie explained that it was a shot to keep me from getting sick. She said her doctor gives her shots too and that it only hurts for a second. Cooper and Dan the Man think I'm tough but I didn't like shots much. It was true; they did only hurt for a second but the thought of having them was worse than the actual shot. I was a little afraid to go back to Dr. Mike.

"Don't be afraid, Stewy Baby. I'll be there to hold your paw." Katie nuzzled me and kissed my owie.

"Okay guys, get ready for school. I don't have a lot of cheesecakes to bake today so I'll pick you up at school, then we'll take Stewy to the doctors," Kristi said.

"It's a good thing we're taking her in; it looks like she has a third eye." Cooper placed his fist between his eyes, pretending to be me. "Look everyone, Stewy and I are twin super heroes with the ability to see all things great and small." Cooper zoomed through the kitchen pretending to be my third eye super hero twin. "It's the amazing Stewarto and Super Cooper ready to conquer the world." Cooper was buzzing around the kitchen in his superhero cape.

If this is what being a superhero felt like, Cooper could have it.

CHAPTER 8

The Dreaded Cone

B Y THE TIME Kristi and the kids got home to take me to Dr. Mike's my third eye had gotten so big it had swollen my left eye shut. My head was throbbing and I didn't even feel like getting into the garbage cans or eating flip flops. Something was definitely wrong with me.

"Oh my gosh Mommy look at poor Stewy Baby, her eye is swollen shut," Katie sobbed. "What if she goes blind?"

Blind? What was blind? I looked at Katie with my good eye and cocked my head. She knew what I was thinking and explained to me.

"Blind is when you can't see out of your eyes anymore Stewy. But don't worry we would never let that happen to you."

"She doesn't even look like a superhero anymore," Cooper said "Do you think she'll go blind Mom?"

"No, Stewy will be just fine. Don't worry guys, Dr. Mike will fix her up," Kristi reassured the kids. "Don't worry Stewy, you're not going blind."

We loaded up into Kristi's boxy car and drove to Dr. Mike's. I laid my gross head on Katie's lap. She stroked it timidly.

When we walked into Dr. Mike's office I was surprised to see a waiting room full of animals and humans. The first time I had come to Dr. Mike's there was just one other dog waiting. This time there was an overweight dog with a hurt paw, a fluffy, little dog shaking on its old human's lap, a great big black dog that was the size of a pony, two cats in cages and a little rodent that looked like a mouse. Katie called it a hamster. I felt a special bond with all of these other animals. We had one thing in common, none of us wanted to be there. Dr. Mike was a nice guy and all, but he used sharp poky things that didn't really feel that great.

I walked over to the old human with the shaking dog on her lap. I sniffed the

fluffy dog and licked her human's hand trying to reassure her that everything was going to be fine.

"This is Stewy Baby," Katie said to the old human, "She's very scared right now. She's afraid that she's going to go blind. What's wrong with your doggie?"

"Ohhhhh, Sophie's just old," The old lady said in a shaking voice. "She's not feeling well, I'm afraid she's not going to be with us much longer."

Katie was quiet for a moment then said, "Don't worry, Sophie will be just fine. She has lot's more years with you; I know these things."

The old lady smiled at Katie and looked a little less worried.

"Stewy Baby?" a young nurse with a clip board called from the opened door.

"Come on Katie, it's our turn," Kristi called.

"Good luck Stewy Baby, you'll be fine. I know these things too." The old lady smiled at me.

It made me feel a little better.

The young nurse placed me on a cold shiny table. I didn't like this table the first time I was here and I didn't like it now. My little puppy paws couldn't get a grip on that thing; they just kind of slid around awkwardly. Someone should really let the animal doctors know that these tables didn't work out for us.

"Well hello Stewy Baby, fancy meeting you here," Dr. Mike laughed. "Looks like you have a big knot on your head."

"Stewy Baby got in a fight with Charlie, the neighborhood cat. He's a big bully. He was trying to eat her friend the magpie. Stewy saved the magpie but apparently, Charlie chomped her a good one," Katie informed Dr. Mike.

"Yeah, the amazing Stewarto lost that battle," Cooper said.

"We think it might be infected," Kristi chimed in.

"Well Stewy Baby, it looks like you saved the day. Unfortunately I think Kristi might be right, it looks like an abscess to me." Dr. Mike pressed on my head. I whimpered.

"Will you have to drain it with a needle?" Cooper asked full of excitement.

"Yes, I'll have to drain it," Dr. Mike answered.

"Will puss and blood come out?" Cooper asked.

"Probably," Dr. Mike said.

"That's awesome! Can I watch?" Cooper asked.

"Sure, if you want to." Dr. Mike was taking my temperature and looking in my eyes.

"Cool!" Cooper said.

"Can I be there too?" Katie asked "I hate puss and blood but Stewy's scared. I need to hold her paw."

"You have two very brave kids," Dr. Mike said to Kristi.

"Yes I do, but I'm afraid they don't have a very brave mother. I don't do puss and blood. I'll stay in here," Kristi said.

We followed Dr. Mike into another room, where he set me up on another cold, shiny, slick table.

"Be brave Stewy. It should only hurt for a second," Katie said holding my paw.

Hurt for a second? I didn't want it to hurt at all.

"Cooooooooooool" Cooper said as Dr. Mike inserted the needle into my third eye.

"Just as I thought, it's an abscess," Dr. Mike said as he carried me back into Kristi. "I'm afraid we'll have to perform surgery and place a drain tube in it."

"Surgery? Does that mean you'll have to put her under?" Kristi asked.

"I'm afraid so, this is a pretty bad abscess, and with it being so close to her eye I worry about it affecting her eyesight. We'll do the surgery this afternoon then keep her overnight," Dr. Mike said.

"Poor Stewy, poor, poor Stewy," Katie said.

"She'll have to wear a cone around her head and you'll have to keep her quiet for about a week," Dr. Mike explained.

Surgery, a drain tube and a cone around my head? I was beginning to wonder if Marge had been worth it. Life had been so much easier in the barn.

CHAPTER 9

Home Again, Home Again Joggity Jog

WHEN I WOKE up from my surgery the next morning I felt sooooooo strange. All of the dogs in the cages around me seemed to be speaking in slow motion. I lifted my head to see who was in the room with me but I couldn't see anything. My head was surrounded by something white and plastic. Could this be the dreaded cone?

"Yo, Stewy Baby. You awake?" a deep voice echoed in my plastic device.

"Yeah, sort of." I moved my head to the left to try to see who was talking but my

cone hit the side of the kennel and I got stuck. I pried my head back and released the cone. I couldn't see anything around me, only straight ahead.

"Man, you are in bad shape girl," the deep voice said.

"Who are you and what's on my head?" I asked.

"Name's Joeeeee. I'm a purebred basset hound and you, my friend are sporting the dreaded cone of shame on your head."

"I thought so. I feel like I'm in a foggy tunnel not to mention my head hurts really bad," I whined.

"Girl, you are in a tunnel," Joe laughed. "Half your head is shaved and you have a big old ugly tube hanging out of it. Don't worry, the worst of it is over, Dr. Mike fixed you up."

"What happened to you?" I asked.

"I guess you can say I put my nose where it didn't belong," Joe said.

"Where would that be?" I asked.

"A porcupines butt," Joe chuckled again. "Got a face full of quills."

"Ouch, why are you laughing about it?" I asked.

"Well Stewy Baby, I could laugh or I could cry. I choose to laugh."

"You ready to get those quills taken out Joe?" Dr. Mike's assistant, Candy, came in and took Joe out of his cage.

"Good luck Joe, keep laughing," I said. Candy carried Joe by my kennel and I was amazed to see a bunch of pointy things sticking out of Joe's face. How on earth could he laugh about a thing like that?

"Looks like you two have become friends," Candy said to me and Joe. "Your family will be here in a minute to take you home, Stewy."

Thank goodness, I could go home to my family!

A little while later, the fearsome threesome, Katie, Cooper and Kristi, came and picked me up. I had never been so happy to see my special humans. Katie ran to me with tears in her eyes as I was brought out to them.

"Oh Stewy Baby, what have they done to you? I'm so glad you're going to be okay," Katie sobbed.

"That is so awesome!" Cooper yelled. "Check out all that puss oozing out of Stewy's tube."

The great thing about Cooper was the grosser I was, the more he liked me. I never had to worry about my gas, my puss or my vomit around Coop. The grosser the better. I was good with that because it seemed that gross things liked me.

"Does she really have to wear that cone for a week?" Kristi asked.

"I'm afraid so. We don't want her taking that tube out by scratching at it," Candy said.

What would Spud think of my cone of shame? What would Ed think of my cone of shame? I was dreading the thought of having to see both of them; I knew they would laugh at me. I was starting to feel very sorry for myself when I remembered what Joe said, "You could either laugh or cry." Right then and there I chose to be happy about my cone of shame. I was going to make this cone a fun game. I bobbed my head back and forth, the cone bobbed with me. I started spinning circles and cocked my head and barked. I smiled my best canine smile.

"Check out Stewy, she's doing the cone dance," Cooper said pointing to me.

"Stewy's happy that Dr. Mike fixed her and she can still see," Katie said. "I'm going to color Stewy's cone pink, then it will just look like a big fancy collar."

"Not another pink thing!" Cooper groaned.

"Are you happy to be going home Stewy?" Kristi asked.

I barked and spun another circle. Was I ever!

"What was that dumb song you were singing on the way over?" Cooper asked Katie.

"TO DOCTOR TO DOCTOR

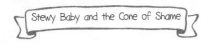

TO PICK UP MY DOG
HOME AGAIN, HOME AGAIN
JOGGITY JOG!" Katie sang.

Kristi and Cooper laughed and repeated Katie's funny lyrics.

"TO DOCTOR TO DOCTOR
TO PICK UP MY DOG
HOME AGAIN HOME AGAIN
JOGGITY JOG." They both sang.

I pranced out of Dr. Mike's with my cone head held high. Home again, home again joggity jog.

CPSIA information can be obtained
at www.ICGtesting.com
Printed in the USA
FSHW020013141021